D1137844

This Little Tiger book belongs to:

_____

_____

_____

For Sam, who taught me
everything I know about bees
~ S S

For my BEEootiful
BaBEE, Levi
~ J T

LITTLE TIGER PRESS
An imprint of Magi Publications
1 The Coda Centre, 189 Munster Road,
London SW6 6AW
www.littletigerpress.com

First published in Great Britain 2007
This edition published 2012

Text copyright © Steve Smallman 2007
Illustrations copyright © Jack Tickle 2007
Steve Smallman and Jack Tickle have asserted
their rights to be identified as the author and
illustrator of this work under the Copyright,
Designs and Patents Act, 1988
A CIP catalogue record for this book
is available from the British Library
All rights reserved
ISBN 978-1-84895-280-5

Printed in China

LTP/1800/0303/1011

10 9 8 7 6 5 4 3 2 1

The Very

Greedy Bee

Steve Smallman   **Jack Tickle**

LITTLE TIGER PRESS
London

In a busy, buzzy beehive lived a very greedy bee.
All the other bees worked hard making honey
and cleaning the hive, but the Greedy Bee spent
all day gobbling pollen and guzzling nectar.
SLURP! SLURP! BURP!

Eeek!

The Greedy Bee wouldn't share
his nectar with anyone.
He wouldn't even let a tired
ladybird sit on his flower.
"Find your own flower!" he
shouted. "This one is **MINE!**"

And when, one day, the Greedy Bee
found a meadow full of the biggest,
juiciest flowers he had ever seen,
he decided not to tell **ANYONE!**
  "**YUMMY!**" he buzzed. "Lots and
lots of flowers and they're all for **ME!**"

The Greedy Bee whizzed
and bizzed from flower
to flower, slurping and
burping, and growing
FATTER...

and **FATTER**...

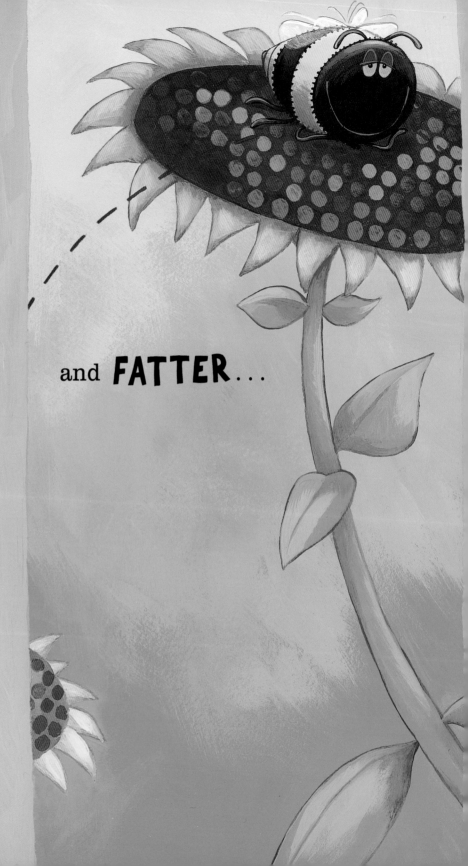

and **FATTER**...

and **FATTER!**

At last his tummy was full and he settled down on a big pink flower in the warm yellow sunshine and fell fast asleep.

z z z z z z z z z !

When the Greedy Bee woke up,
it was **DARK**. He tried to fly,
but his tummy was so stodgy
and podgy that . . .

he went down instead
of up and landed,
BIFF! BANG! THUMP!
on the ground below.

"**I'M SCARED!**" cried the Greedy Bee,

"and I don't know how to get home!"

Then he saw two glowing eyes in the long grass.

"**EEK!**" he cried. "A **MONSTER** is coming to eat me!"

But it wasn't a monster, it was two friendly
fireflies, their bottoms glowing in the dark.
"What's wrong?" they asked.
"I'm too full to fly," wailed the Greedy Bee,
"and I can't walk home in the dark!"

"Follow us," said the fireflies, and they
all set off on the long, long journey home.

Through forests
of flowers and
squelchy mud . . .

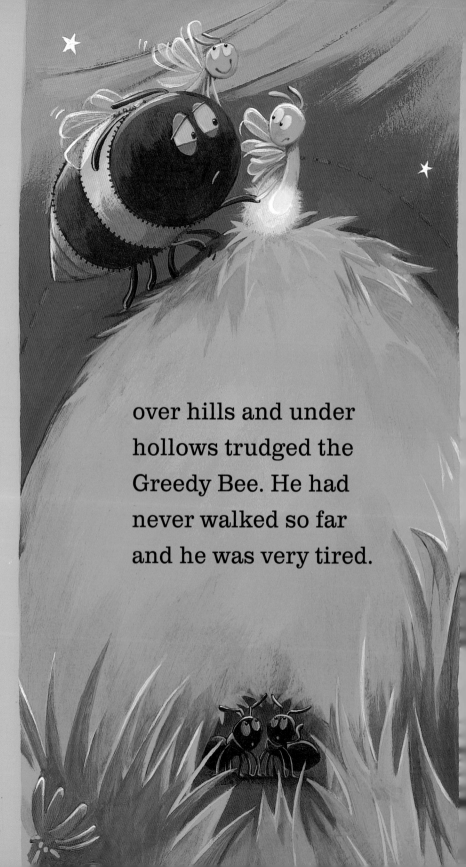

over hills and under
hollows trudged the
Greedy Bee. He had
never walked so far
and he was very tired.

"Soon be there!"
called the
fireflies kindly.

Then they heard
a whooshing,
watery noise . . .

"Ha ha! I'm almost home!" cried the
Greedy Bee excitedly. "It's the stream!"
And it was, but his hive was on
the other side of it.

"Oh dear," cried the Greedy Bee, flopping down with a flump on the floor. "How will I ever get across?" he sniffled sadly.

"We'll help you!" said a tiny ant with a big leaf.

The ant and his friends flipped
one of their leaves into the water.
    "Jump in!" they cried.
Then, helped by the fireflies,
the Greedy Bee and the ants
made their way, splishing and
splashing, over to the other side
of the stream.

"**HOORAY, I'M HOME!**" cried the Greedy Bee.

"Wherever have you been?" called the other bees.

"**I OVERSLURPED!**" said the Greedy Bee. "I would never have got home if my new friends hadn't been so kind, so now I'm going to share my best honey with them. Would you like some too?"

"Great!" said the other bees. "Let's have a party!"

Everyone tucked
into a midnight feast of
yummy, runny honey.
All except for one **VERY**
sleepy, **VERY** happy,
but **NOT** so greedy bee!

Eat your way through more delicious titles from Little Tiger Press!

PICTURE BOOK and CD SET

QUIET!

Paul Bright

illustrated by
Guy Parker-Rees

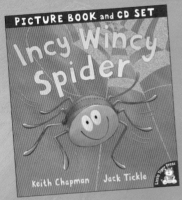

PICTURE BOOK and CD SET

Incy Wincy Spider

Keith Chapman   Jack Tickle

PICTURE BOOK and CD SET

One Winter's Day

M Christina Butler

Illustrated by
Tina Macnaughton

PICTURE BOOK and CD SET

Snow Friends

M Christina Butler and Tina Macnaughton

PICTURE BOOK and CD SET

DIRTY BERTIE

David Roberts

PICTURE BOOK and CD SET

Smelly Peter
The Great Pea Eater

Steve Smallman

Joëlle Dreidemy

For information regarding any of the above titles
or for our catalogue, please contact us:
Little Tiger Press, 1 The Coda Centre,
189 Munster Road, London SW6 6AW
Tel: 020 7385 6333 • Fax: 020 7385 7333
E-mail: info@littletiger.co.uk
www.littletigerpress.com